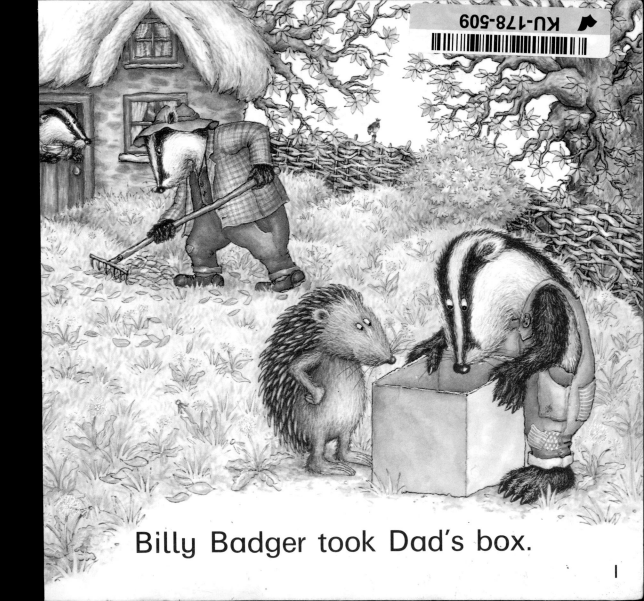

Billy Badger took Dad's box.

1

Hedgehog said, "Let's play."

He got in the box.

3

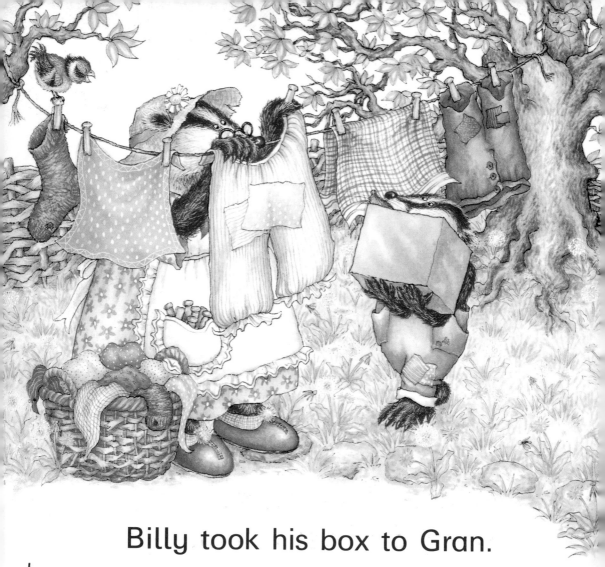

Billy took his box to Gran.

He said, "Look Gran.
There's a monster in my box!"

5

"No," said Gran.
"There's a hedgehog in the box."

Billy took his box to Mum.

He said, "Look Mum.
There's a monster in my box!"

"No," said Mum.
"There's a hedgehog in the box."

Then Dad said, "I want my box."

Billy gave the box to Dad.

Dad shouted, "There's a monster in the box!" And Dad ran away!